D0653518

This book belongs to

This edition published by Parragon Books Ltd in 2017

Parragon Books Ltd
Chartist House
15–17 Trim Street
Bath BA1 1HA, UK
www.parragon.com

ISBN 978-1-4748-8323-8

Printed in China

MARVEL COLLECTION

MARVEL THOR™

Parragon

Bath • New York • Cologne • Melbourne • Delhi
Hong Kong • Shenzhen • Singapore

What would it be like to live among gods? To be something more than human? To hold great power in your hands and know how to use it? To be brave? To be honoured? To be mighty?

This is a story about someone who was born into royalty but needed to earn his honour. This is a story about a hero named THOR.

Thor's realm was called Asgard. It sat like an island where the shores were swept by the sea of space.

The people who lived on Asgard were called Asgardians. The Asgardians called Earth Midgard. The only way to reach Earth from Asgard was by the rainbow bridge, Bifrost. The bridge was guarded by a sentry called Heimdall.

Even though Asgard was well protected, threats were endless. Thor was one of the land's greatest protectors.

Thor was also a prince. He lived with his brother, Loki, in the castle of their father, Odin.

Thor was arrogant and chose his friends for their loyalty: the brave warrior Balder, a band of soldiers called the Warriors Three – Fandral, Volstagg and Hogun – and the beautiful, strong and wise Lady Sif.

Thor's father, Odin, ruled over all of Asgard. He and his wife, Frigga, wanted nothing more than for their sons to grow up to be just and worthy rulers.

But there could only be one supreme ruler of Asgard. Only one who could be like Odin. And even though Loki was thoughtful, clever and quick ...

… Thor was firstborn and so the throne was his by right.

To decide when Thor would be ready to rule, Odin had a special hammer made. It was forged from a mystical metal called Uru, which came from the heart of a dying star. The hammer was named Mjolnir and it held great power.

But no one would be able to lift the
hammer unless he or she was worthy.

And the hammer was immovable to Thor.

Still, Odin's actions made it clear: the hammer was meant for his firstborn son and no one else.

Even so, proving worthy of Mjolnir was not an easy task. Thor spent nearly every moment trying to earn his right to hold the hammer.

The young prince performed amazing acts of bravery.

Thor was honoured by the people of Asgard for acts of nobility.

In battle, he demonstrated feats of great strength …

… and honour.

With every great achievement, Thor attempted once more to pick up Mjolnir. But it seemed as if he would never raise the hammer more than a few centimetres from the ground. Until one day …

… he DID!

Thor had proven himself worthy of his weapon and he used it well. When he threw the hammer, it always returned to him.

When he twirled it by its handle, he could soar like a winged beast!
And when he slammed it twice upon the ground …

… he could summon all
the power of lightning,
rain and thunder!

In fact, with his hammer in hand, there was little Thor could not do.

Odin wanted Thor to be a great warrior and he had become one. He wanted him to earn the respect of Asgard – he had it. But Thor began to let the power go to his head. And Odin was not happy. In fact, he had grown quite angry with his son.

Odin told Thor that he was his favoured son. He told him that he was brave beyond compare and noble as a prince must be. He told him that his strength was legendary and that he was the best warrior in the kingdom.

But Thor did not know what it meant to be weak or to feel pain. And without knowing humility, Thor could never be a truly honourable warrior.

Odin was angry. In his rage, he tore Mjolnir from Thor's hand and threw it towards Midgard. Then he stripped Thor of his armour and sent him to Earth.

Odin made his son believe that he was a medical student named Don Blake, with an injured leg.

As Blake, Thor learned to study hard. At times he thought he might fail. But he worked harder than he ever had in Asgard and, in the end, he earned his degree.

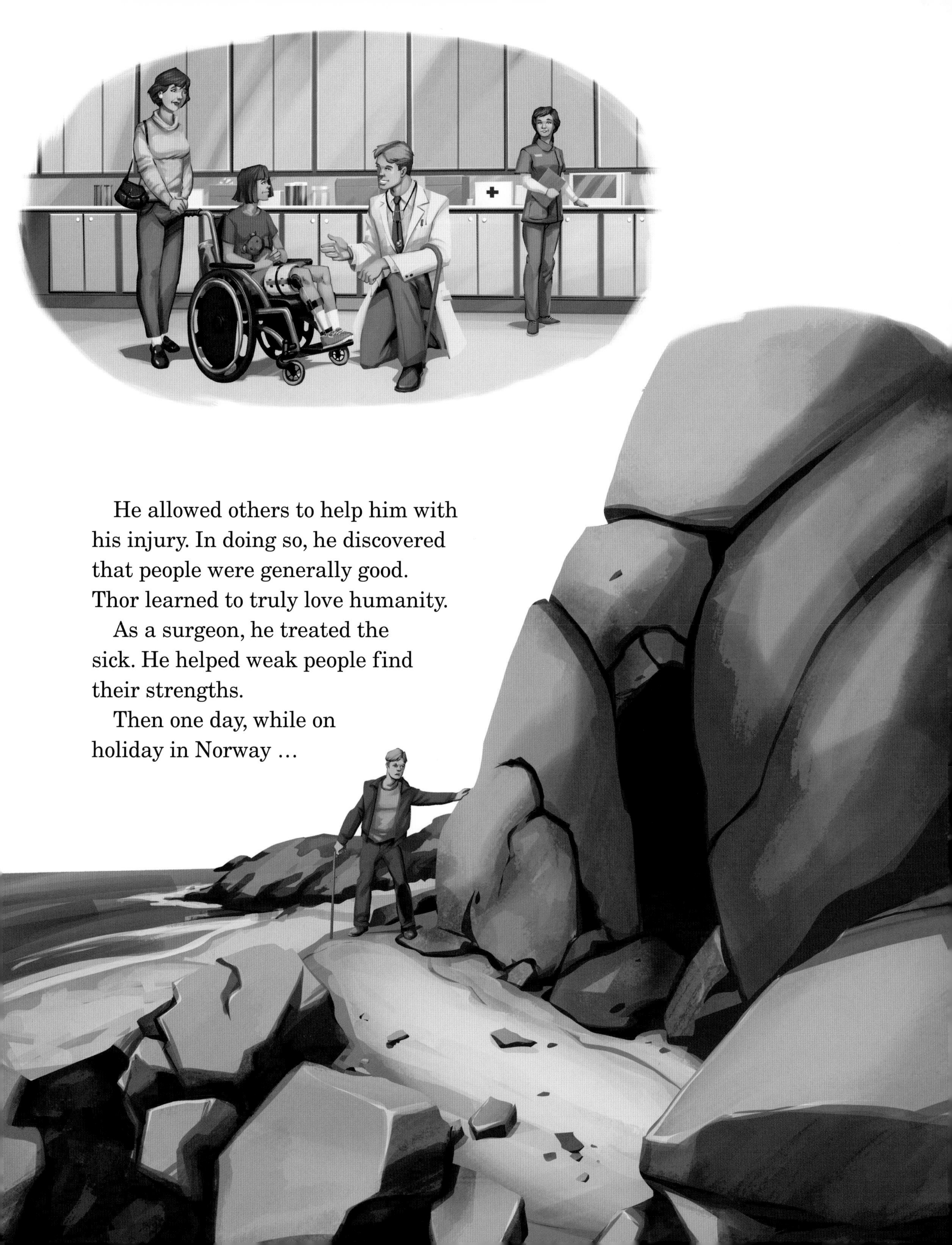

He allowed others to help him with his injury. In doing so, he discovered that people were generally good. Thor learned to truly love humanity.

As a surgeon, he treated the sick. He helped weak people find their strengths.

Then one day, while on holiday in Norway …

… Don Blake became trapped in a cave after a huge boulder blocked the only possible exit.

He found a staff on the ground and shoved it under the boulder. He tried with all his might to move the rock. He pushed and pushed – nothing.

Don was so angry that he took the staff and struck it on the ground. But this was no ordinary stick….

It was Mjolnir in disguise!

Odin had sent Don to this cave. The Allfather of Asgard was pleased.

His son had, at last, become a true hero. He had become human in spirit, but still, now and forever, he was ...

... THE MIGHTY THOR.

MARVEL COLLECTION

Bruce Banner was
not always strong.

He was not always powerful.

And he was not always able to do incredible things.

But most of all, Bruce was not always feared.

In fact, when he was young, Bruce was mostly afraid.

He was often sad and nervous, and he didn't have a lot of friends. But he was always ready to help someone in need.

Bruce kept all his feelings buried deep inside him. Reading books about science always took his mind off things.

And so, Bruce spent an awful lot of time with those books.

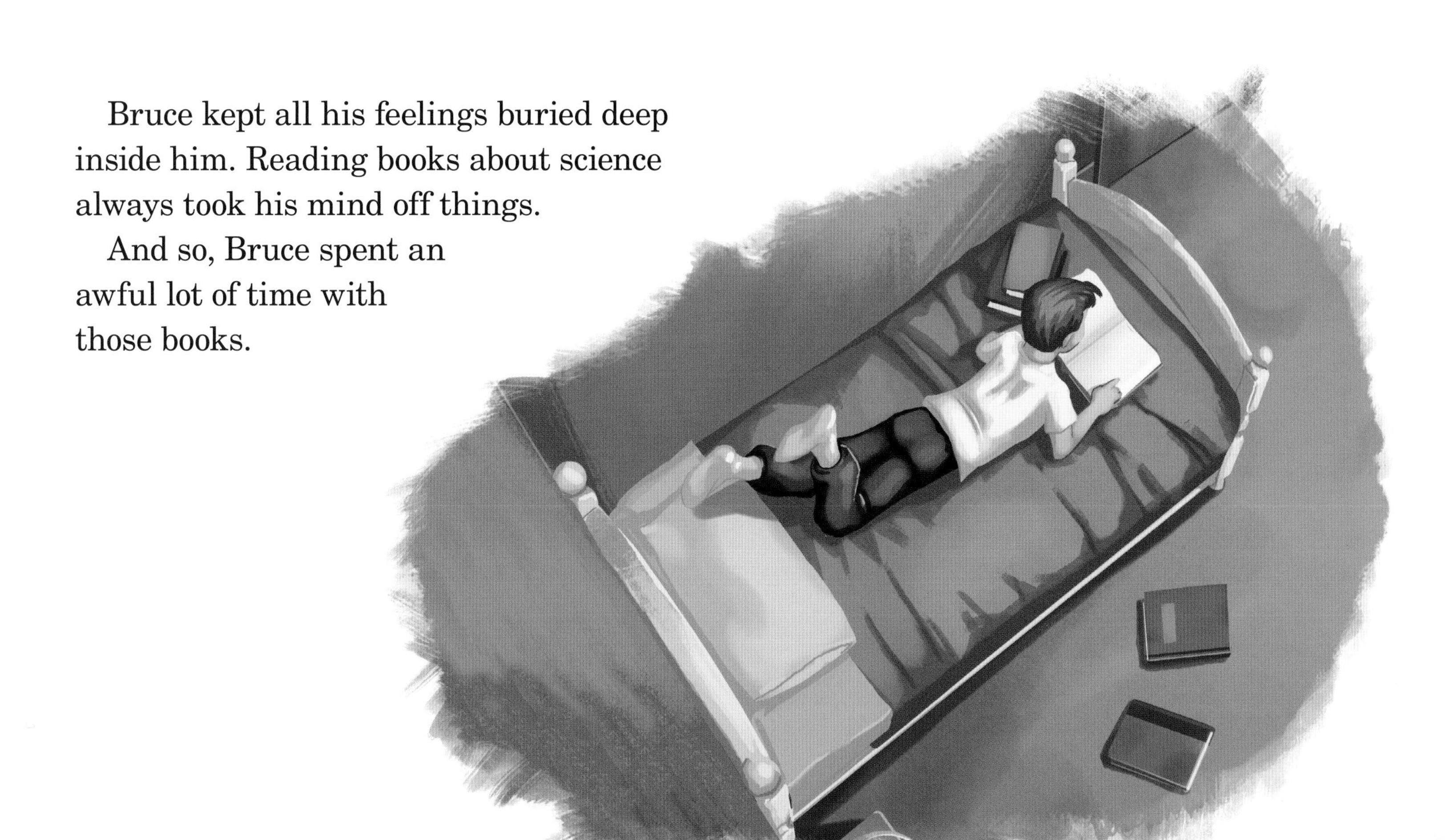

As Bruce grew older he continued to read, study and learn ... but he never understood how to talk about his feelings.

Bruce became a doctor of science who worked for the army. He worked very hard both day and night.

He was studying a type of energy called GAMMA RADIATION. It was very dangerous, so he needed to be careful when he was near it. He wanted to find a way to use its power for good.

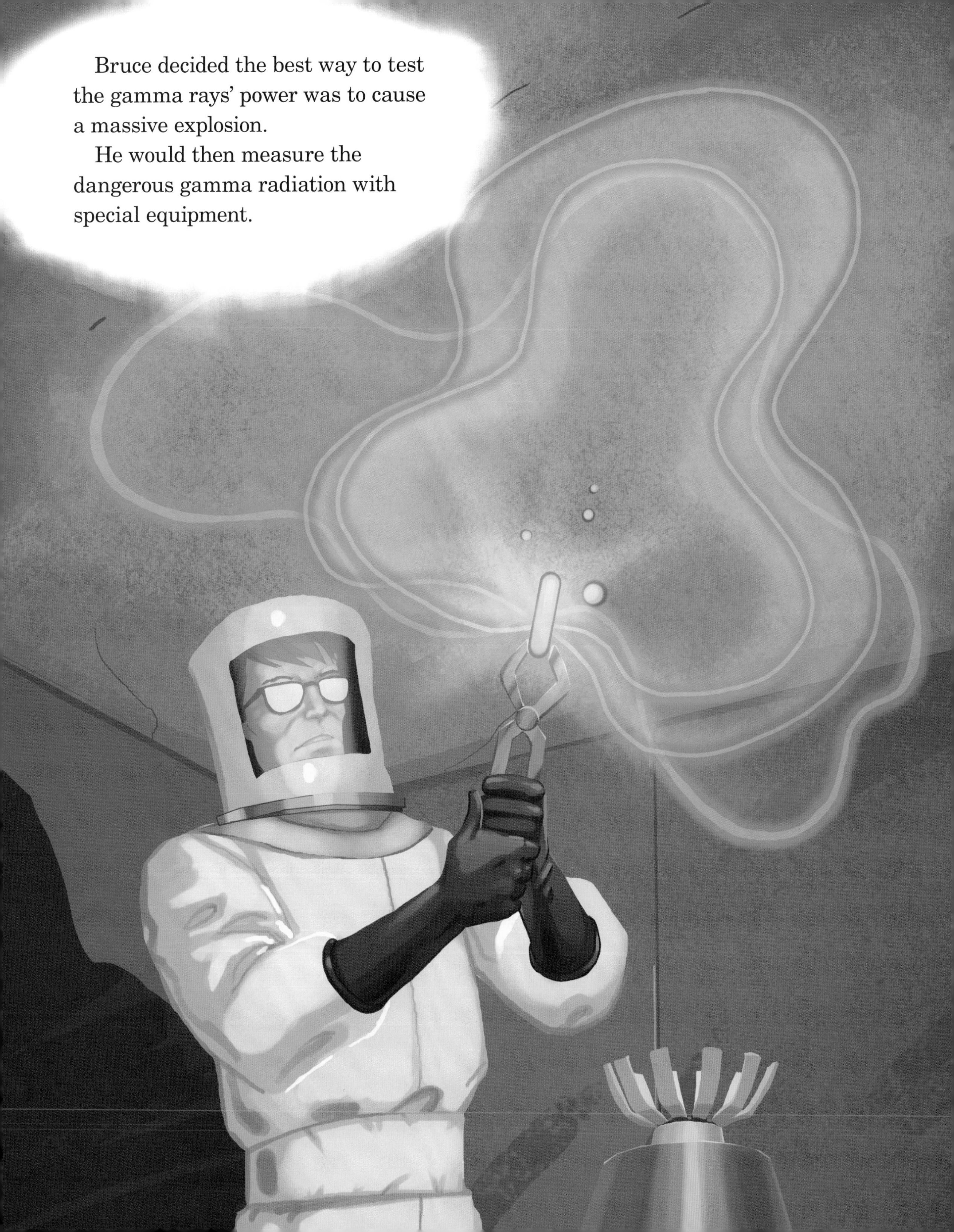

Bruce decided the best way to test the gamma rays' power was to cause a massive explosion.

He would then measure the dangerous gamma radiation with special equipment.

General 'Thunderbolt' Ross was in charge of the army lab where Bruce worked. The general was angry with Bruce because he had been waiting far too long to find out how much power the gamma rays held.

But Bruce needed time to make sure the device was safe. He didn't want anyone to get hurt. This made General Ross even angrier, so he yelled at Bruce.

Bruce remembered how upset he felt when people yelled at him when he was a kid. So he listened to the general's orders and sent the device to a safe area in the desert to be tested.

Soon, the countdown began.

Suddenly, Bruce noticed something strange on his computer screen. He looked through his telescope to see what was wrong.

Someone had driven right into the danger zone!

Bruce rushed out of the lab. He couldn't let anyone be hurt by his experiment.

Bruce told the teenager in the car that he needed to leave the site RIGHT AWAY.

But Bruce quickly realized they did not have time to clear the area!

He pushed the boy to safety inside a nearby shelter.

5 ... 4 ... 3 ...

2 ... 1...

SAFE SH

Bruce woke up in an army hospital.

The teenager was there, too. Bruce learned the boy's name was Rick Jones. Rick thanked Bruce for saving his life.

Bruce was happy that Rick was safe.

He was also happy to be alive.

But then he looked around. He realized that he was locked up, because he had been exposed to the deadly gamma rays. He remembered the blast. He felt so scared, so confused and so helpless. Just the way he had when he was young. Bruce felt trapped.

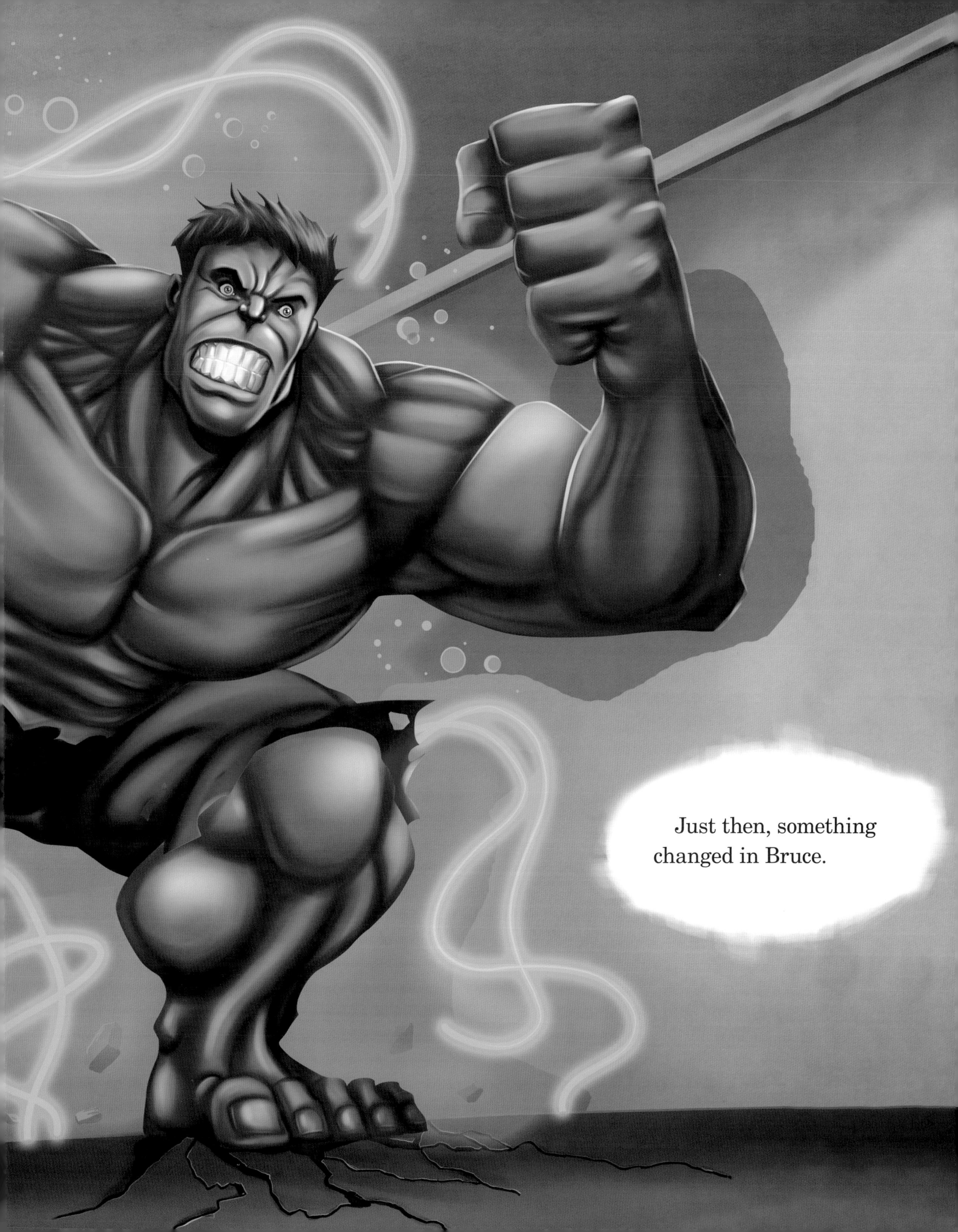

Just then, something changed in Bruce.

The soldiers didn't know that the gamma rays had transformed Bruce! They didn't recognize him. They called him a HULK!

The army tried to stop the Hulk. But the Hulk just wanted to leave.

He didn't want to hurt anyone. He only wanted to be left alone.

So when he noticed that his actions had put the soldiers in harm's way ...

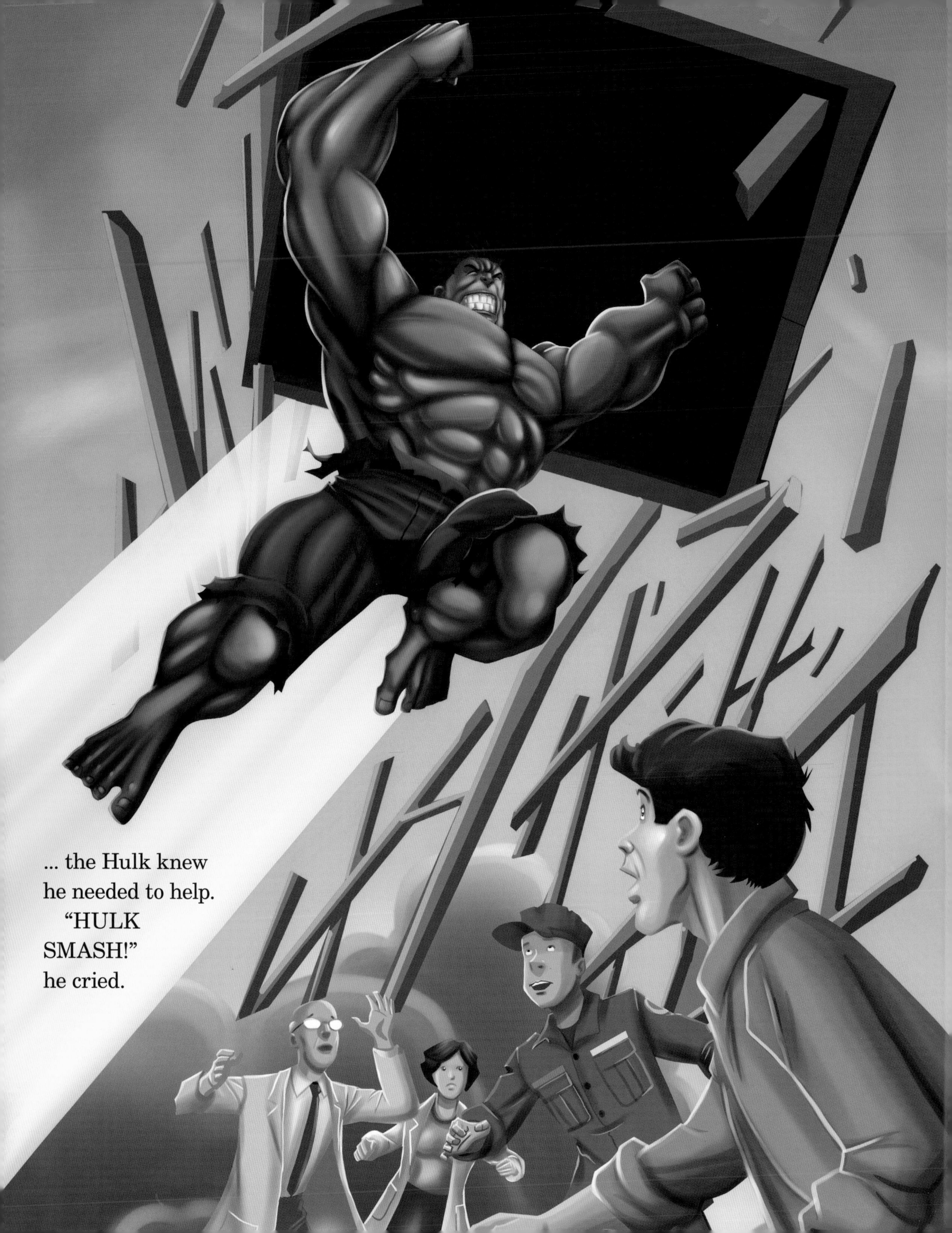

... the Hulk knew
he needed to help.

"HULK
SMASH!"
he cried.

The Hulk had saved the soldiers!

Then he leaped away before he could do any more damage.

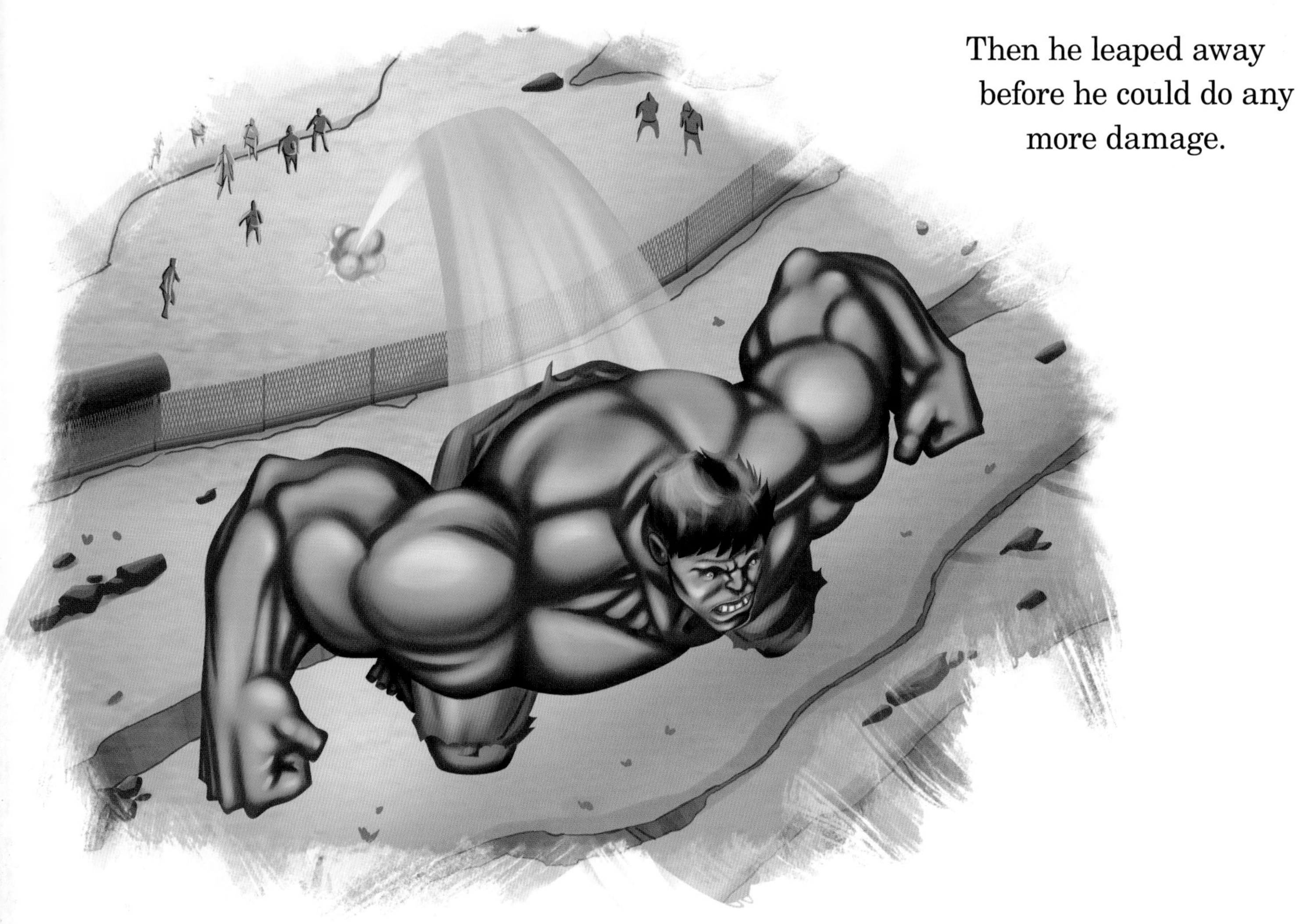

Not long after, he transformed back into Bruce Banner.

Bruce didn't know if he would ever change into the Hulk again. But he thought it best to hide out and lie low – just in case.

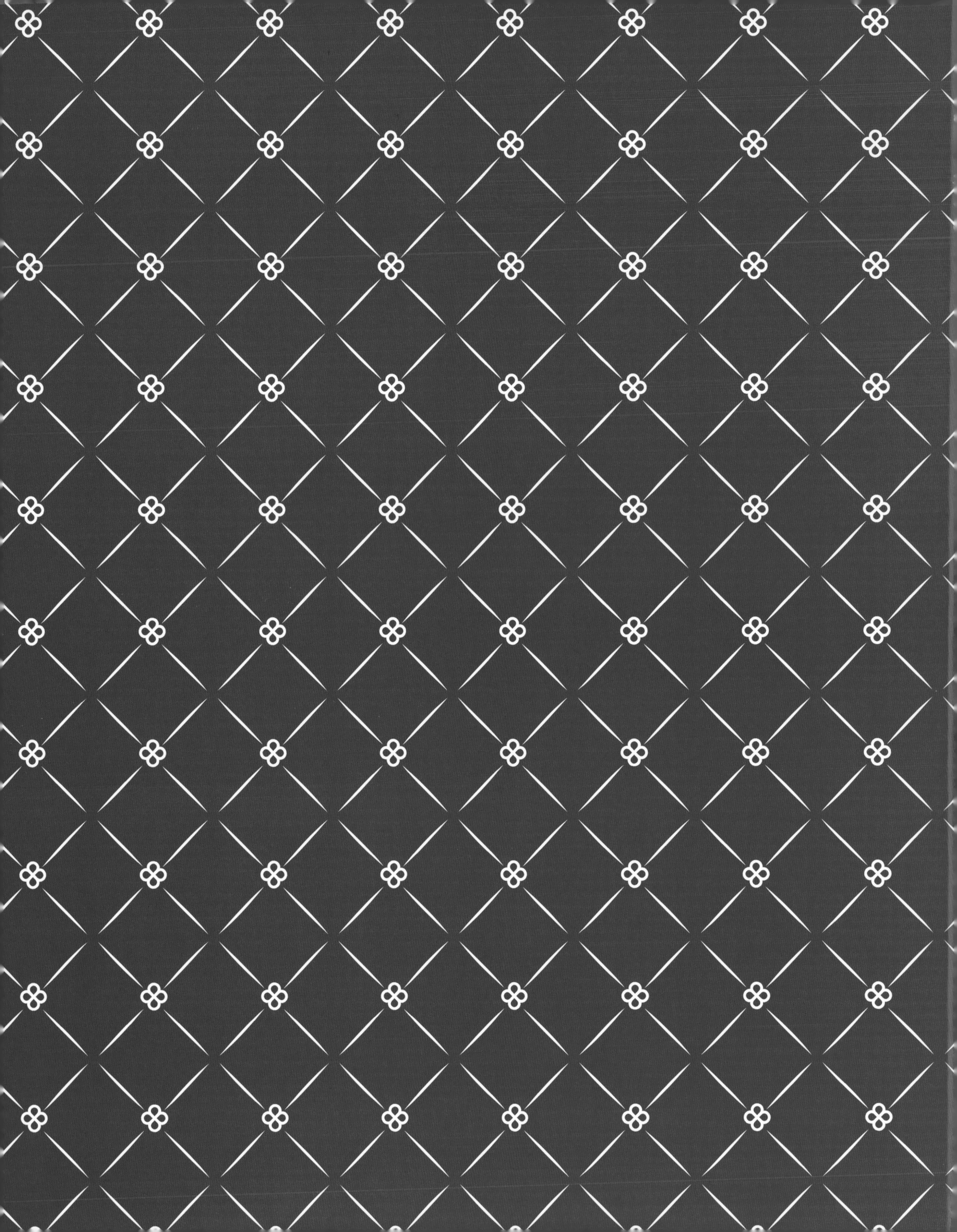

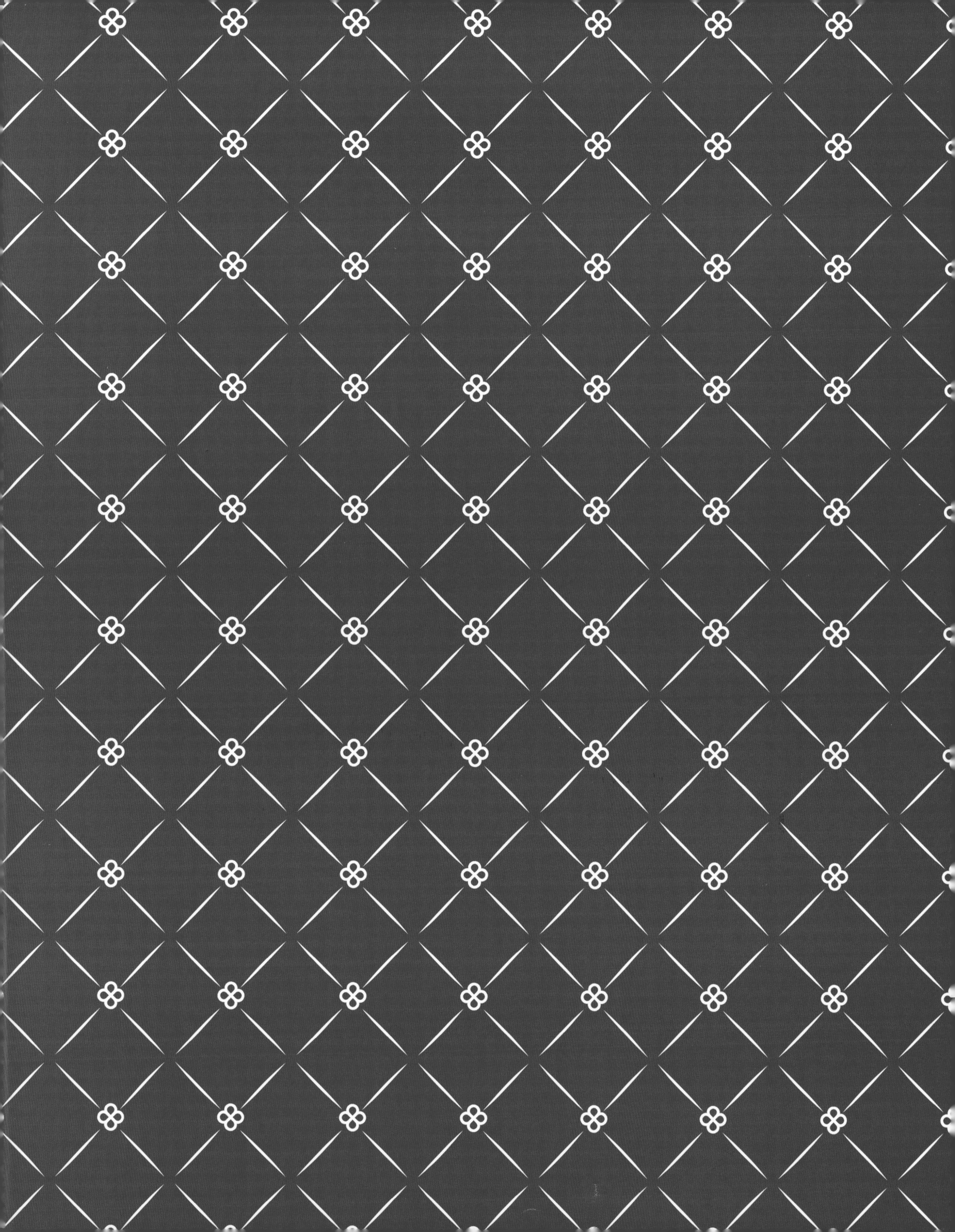

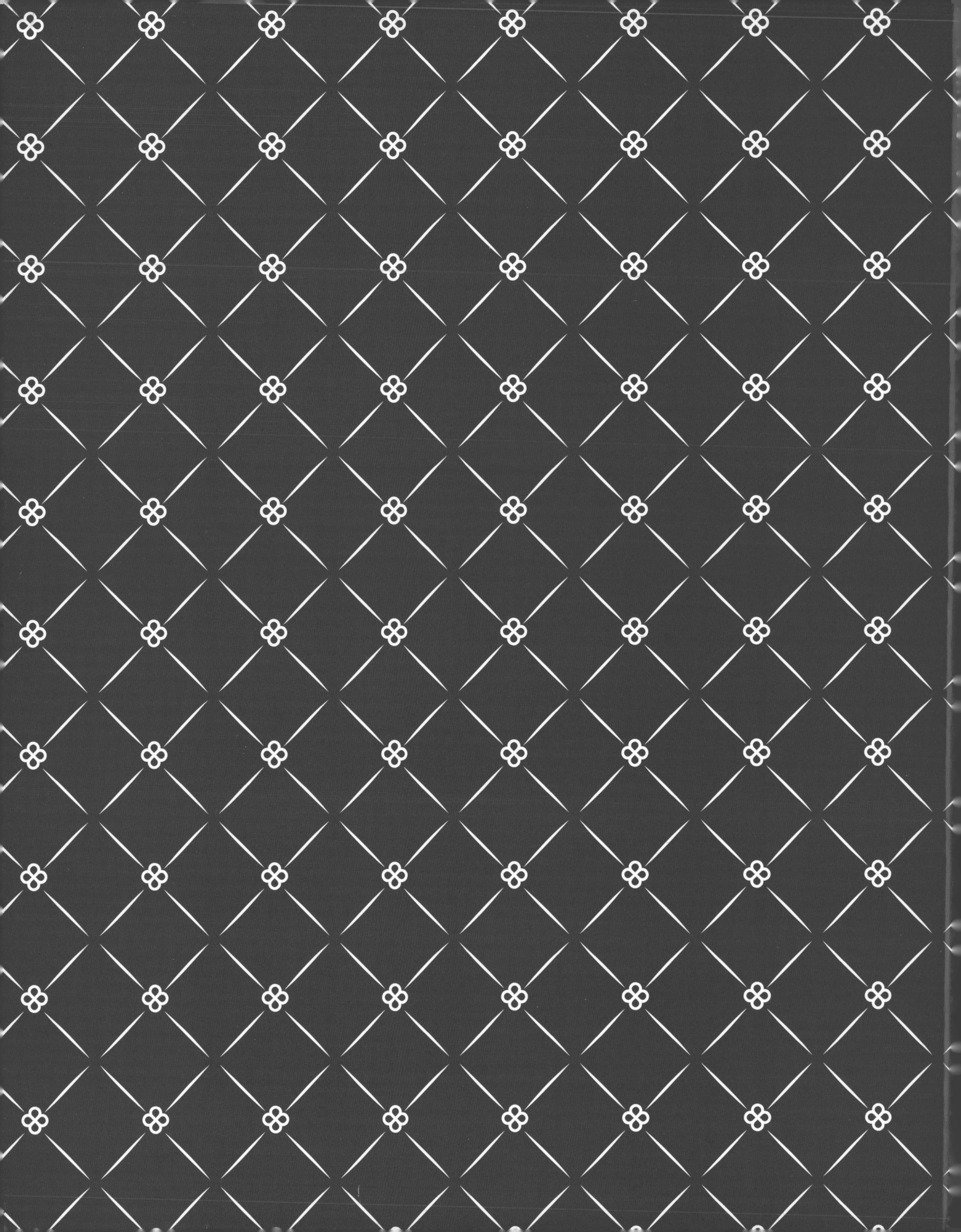